THE UNIVERSE

OUR GALAXY, "THE MILKY WAY"

OUR SOLAR SYSTEM

OUR PLANET, EARTH, AND SATELITE, MOON

HEMISPHERE

CONTINENT

COUNTRY

STATE

CITY

STREET

HOUSE

Special thanks to Andrew Knoll, Fisher Professor of Natural History at Harvard University, for his invaluable assistance in updating the information in this book.

Printed in China
RNF ISBN 978-0-547-19508-7
PAP ISBN 978-0-547-20359-1

SCP 10 9 8 7 6 5
4500503675

LIFE STORY

The story of Life on our Earth from its beginning up to now.

NARRATORS: An Astronomer, a Geologist, a Paleontologist, a Historian, a Grandmother, and VIRGINIA LEE BURTON

LEADING ANIMALS	LEADING PLANTS
(In order of appearance)	(In order of appearance)
TRILOBITES	SEAWEEDS
CEPHALOPODS	MOSS PLANTS
SEA SCORPIONS	FERNS
FISH	CLUB MOSSES
AMPHIBIANS	HORSE TAILS
REPTILES	SCALE TREES
DINOSAURS	CONIFERS
BIRDS	CYCADS
MAMMALS	FLOWERING PLANTS
HUMANS	GRASSES
DOMESTIC ANIMALS	CULTIVATED PLANTS

OTHERS: Protozoa, sponges, jelly fish and corals, worms (round, flat, and segmented), brachiopods, sea lilies and star fish, mollusks, crabs, lobsters, millipedes, spiders, and insects. Bacteria, fungi, and lichen.

(Note: All plants and animals on stage are drawn to the same scale as the narrators.)

SYNOPSIS OF SCENES

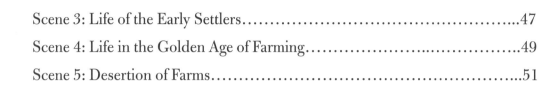

ACT V

MOST RECENT LIFE

Eons and eons ago our Sun was born,
one of the millions and billions of stars
that make up our galaxy, called the Milky Way.
Our galaxy is one of the millions and billions and trillions
of galaxies whirling around in space, which make up the Universe.
Our Sun is not the biggest star, nor is it the smallest,
but to us it is the most important star of all—for
without the light and warmth from our Sun
no Life could live on our Earth.

OUR GALAXY, THE MILKY WAY

OUR SUN

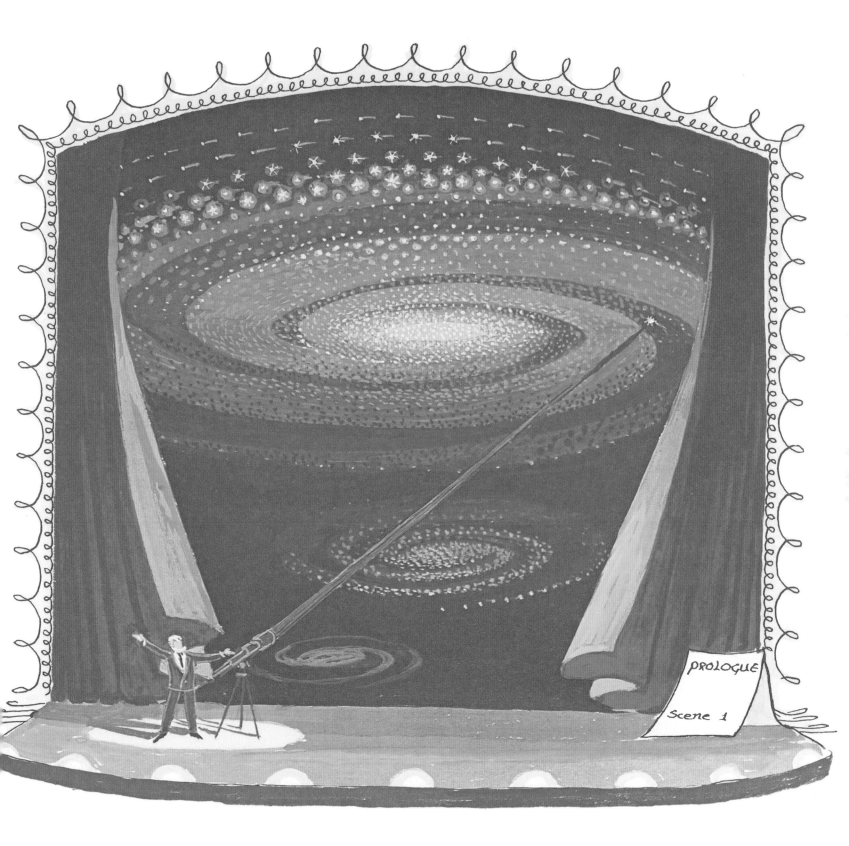

SUN
Diam. 865,000 miles

EARTH
Diameter 7,926 miles

MERCURY
Diam. 3,032 miles

VENUS
Diam. 7,521 miles

MARS
Diam. 4,222 miles

JUPITER
Diam. 88,846 miles

SATURN
Diam. 75,000 miles

URANUS
Diam. 31,800 miles

NEPTUNE
Diam. 30,800 miles

Our Earth was born
millions and billions of years ago,
one of our Sun's family of eight planets.
Our Earth is the third planet out from the Sun.
It is not the biggest planet, nor is it the smallest,
but to us it is the most important, for this is where we live.
Our Earth turns once around on its axis every twenty-
four hours, which makes one day, and it takes 365
days (or one year) to travel once around the Sun.
That is how we measure Time.

Thousands of millions of years ago
our Earth was a red-hot fiery ball of matter—
surrounded by clouds of dust and swirling gases—
hurtling through space as it traveled around the Sun
at the speed of 1,100 miles a minute, or 66,000 miles an hour.
There are many and varied theories about how our Moon was born.
Some say it was once a part of our Earth that spun off into space.
Some say it was a separate and smaller ball of matter,
but nobody really knows because there was nobody there.
Anyway, our Moon circles our earth about once a month,
or, to be exact, every 29½ days.

from about 4,560,000,000 years ago

Way back in time
when our Earth was young
no Life could have lived on it.
Its surface was a red-hot sea of lava
and its center was white hot "liquid" rock.
Thick clouds of steam, dust, and gases hid the Sun.
Flaming-hot meteorites from outer space bombarded it.
Hundreds and thousands and millions of years passed by
and gradually the surface of our Earth began to cool.
As it cooled, it hardened into a thin crust of rocks.
Rocks that have solidified from a "liquid" condition
are called igneous rocks, or fire-made rocks.

HADEAN EON

INTRODUCING
IGNEOUS ROCKS

to about 4,000,000,000 years a

from about 4,000,000,000 years ago

Heat from the interior caused
Earth's crust to move across its surface, forming
great high mountains, low valleys, and deep ocean basins.
The ancient rocks were squeezed, pushed, and folded up and down.
Heat and pressure changed them into another kind of rock,
called metamorphic rock, which means "changing in form."
Thick, dense clouds of steam still hid the Sun.
Life may have been present at this time,
but there is no record of it.

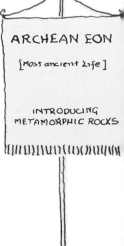

ARCHEAN EON

[Most ancient life]

INTRODUCING
METAMORPHIC ROCKS

To about 2,500,000,000 years ago

from about 2,500,000,000 years ago

From the very beginning,
the clouds opened—rain poured down
in torrents on the now cooled surface of our Earth,
filling the ocean basins and wearing down the mountains.
Rivers and streams carried little particles of rock down
and deposited them in layers on the floors of the oceans.
In time, these layers of sand, gravel, and clay hardened into
rock, called sedimentary rock. Life was present, as was
recorded in fossils of tiny cells and chemical
signatures of the microorganisms
that covered the Earth.

PROTEROZOIC ERA
[Early Life]

INTRODUCING
SEDIMENTARY ROCKS

to about 542,000,000 years ago

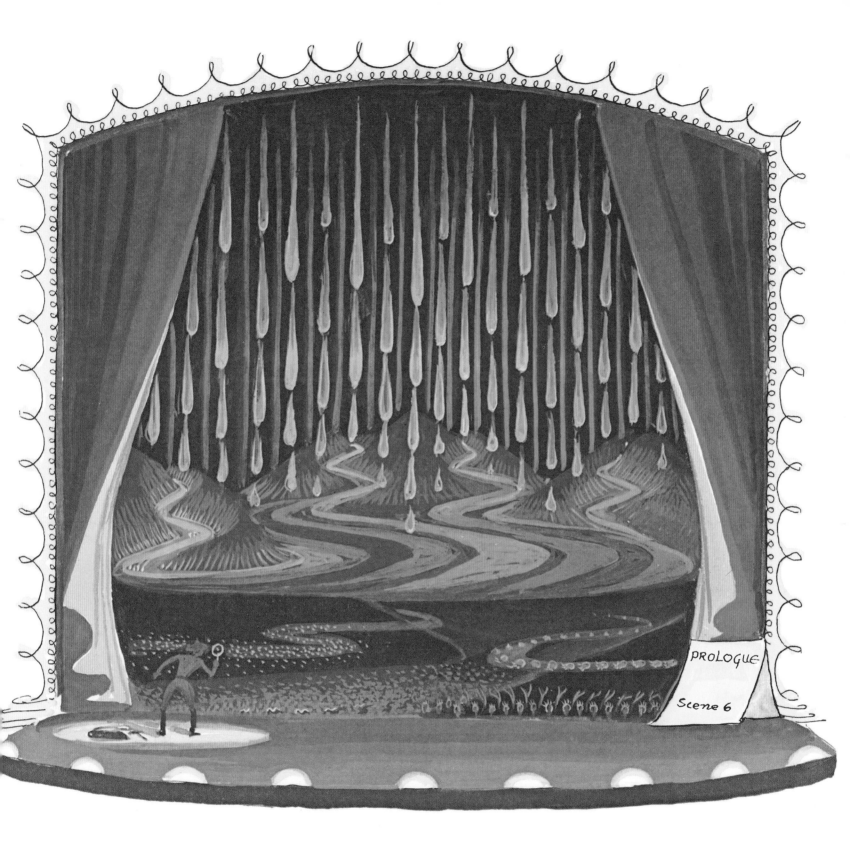

PROLOGUE

Scene 6

from about 542,000,000 years ago

WORMS

CORALS

SEAWEEDS

SEA LILIES

The scene is laid under water.
The story is based on the record of fossils
found in sedimentary rocks half a billion years old.
The ancient Life of this time was made up of sea plants
and little animals without backbones called invertebrates.
The most highly developed of these ancient animals
were the trilobites. They ruled the seas
for a hundred million years.

BRACHIOPODS
brack·e·o·pods

TRILOBITES
try·low·bites

PALEOZOIC ERA
[Ancient Life]

CAMBRIAN
PERIOD

To about 490,000,000 years ago

13

ACT
I

Scene 1

from about 490,000,000 years ago

SNAILS

STARFISH

OSTRACODS

GRAPTOLITES

Life continued
in the warm, shallow seas.
Although there were still trilobites,
their rule was over. Other kinds of invertebrate
sea animals, called cephalopods, now played the leading role.
The name "cephalopod" simply means "having feet on the head."
Squid and octopus of today belong to the same family. Fish,
which first swam in Cambrian oceans, grew more
abundant. Little lichens and simple
mosslike forms lived on land, the
pioneers of the plant world.

PALEOZOIC ERA
[Ancient Life]

ORDOVICIAN
PERIOD

HONEYCOMB
AND HORN CORALS

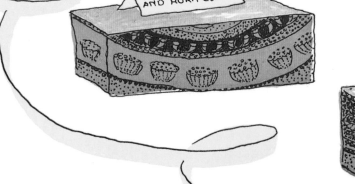

CEPHALOPODS
[seff·a·lo·pods]

to about 444,000,000 years ago

MOSSES

LIVERWORTS

LAND SCORPIONS
AND MILLIPEDES

The scene changed as the land slowly rose.
The seas retreated or evaporated, leaving salt deposits.
On land, the ancestors of liverworts and mosses were joined by
the earliest ancestors of the ferns and seed plants that would later cover
the continents. The cephalopods had decreased in size and in
number. Sea scorpions had taken over the rule of the seas.
More fish appeared on the scene—the first
animals to have backbones,
called vertebrates.

JAWLESS AND
ARMORED FISH

EURYPTERIDS
[you·rip·ter·ids]
OR
SEA SCORPIONS

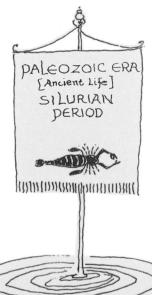

PALEOZOIC ERA
[Ancient Life]
SILURIAN
PERIOD

to about 416,000,000 years ago

17

from about 416,000,000 years ago

FERNS

ANCIENT LUNG FISH

EUSTHENOPTERON [yews·then·op·ter·on]

COCCOSTEUS [ko·kahs·tee·us]

CLADOSELACHE [klad·o·sell·a·key]

Land plants flourished,
clothing our once bare Earth in green.
Ferns made their first appearance at this time,
also early forms of horse tails, club mosses, and scale trees.
These plants instead of creeping along close to the ground
had roots of their own, stems, and leaves, and stood up
reaching for the life-giving warmth and light of our Sun.
Seas, lakes, rivers, and streams swarmed with fish—
big fish, little fish, and medium-sized. A few even
developed lungs and crawled from puddle
to puddle on land. Late in this period,
the first land vertebrates appeared.

PALEOZOIC ERA
[Ancient Life]

DEVONIAN PERIOD

DINICHTHYS [dy·nick·this]

to about 359,000,000 years ago

ACT
I

Scene 4

from about 359,000,000 years ago

INSECTS

AMPHIBIANS

While on some parts
of Earth there were glaciers and an ice age,
on much of the planet the land was low, the climate
warm and moist. Great swamp forests covered much of our
Earth. This period is called the Age of Plants or the Coal Age,
because most of the coal we use today comes from these ancient plants.
Amphibians, another kind of vertebrate, appeared on the scene.
They were animals that lived their early life in the water
and their adult life on land, like the frogs of today.
Insects were present and abundant.

SEED FERNS

SIGILLARIA
[sij·il·lay·ree·a]

LEPIDODENDRON
[lep·e·do·den·dron]

CALAMITES
kal·a·my·teez

CORDAITES
cor·da·eye·teez

PALEOZOIC ERA
[Ancient Life]

CARBONIFEROUS
PERIOD

to about 299,000,000 years

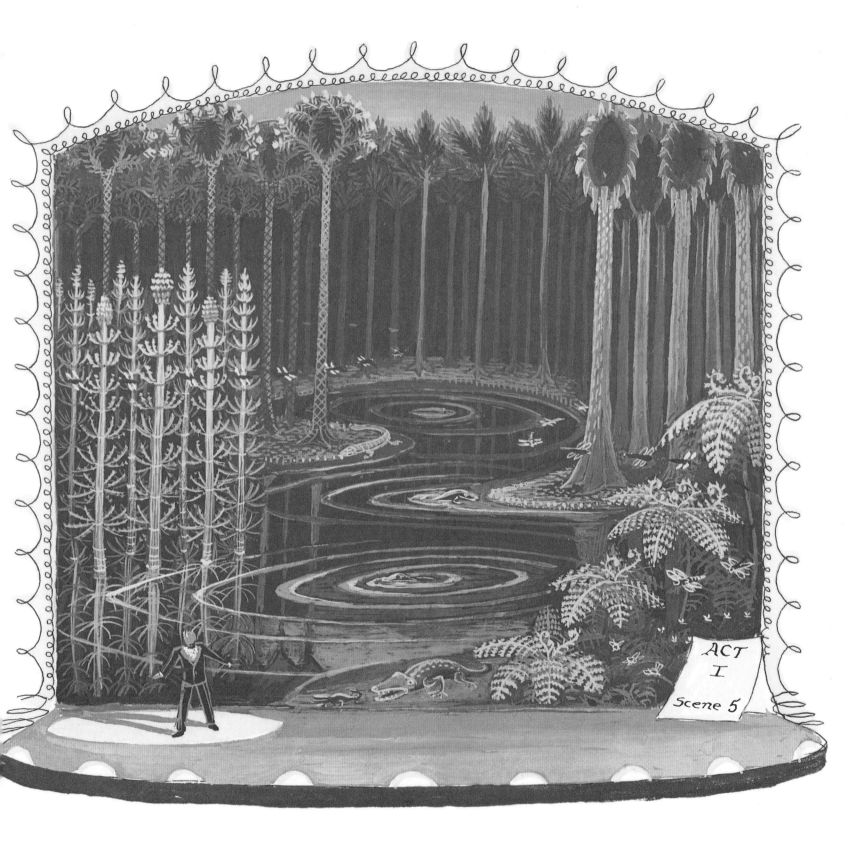

ACT
I
Scene 5

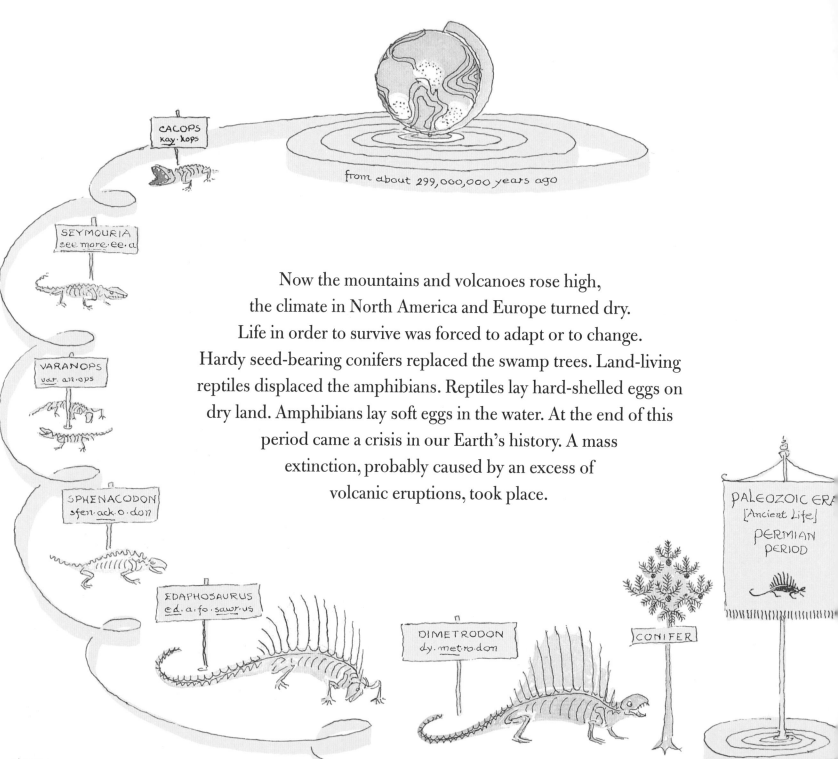

CACOPS
kay·kops

SEYMOURIA
see·more·ee·a

VARANOPS
var·an·ops

SPHENACODON
sfen·ack·o·don

EDAPHOSAURUS
ed·a·fo·sawr·us

DIMETRODON
dy·met·ro·don

CONIFER

PALEOZOIC ERA
[Ancient Life]
PERMIAN
PERIOD

from about 299,000,000 years ago

Now the mountains and volcanoes rose high,
the climate in North America and Europe turned dry.
Life in order to survive was forced to adapt or to change.
Hardy seed-bearing conifers replaced the swamp trees. Land-living
reptiles displaced the amphibians. Reptiles lay hard-shelled eggs on
dry land. Amphibians lay soft eggs in the water. At the end of this
period came a crisis in our Earth's history. A mass
extinction, probably caused by an excess of
volcanic eruptions, took place.

to about 252,000,000 years ago

NOTE:
Meat-eating reptiles in red.
Plant-eating reptiles in green.

ACT
I

Scene 6

from about 252,000,000 years ago

RHYNCHOCEPHALIAN
rink . o . sef . ale . yan

SALTOPOSUCHUS
sal . to . po . sook . us

CYNOGNATHUS
sigh . no . naith . us

PHYTOSAUR
fy . tow . sawr

PLATEOSAURUS
plat . e . o . sawr . us

ICHTHYOSAUR
ich . thee . o . sawr

The climate grew warmer.
Streams and rivers eroded the mountains.
Reptiles continued to play the leading roles.
Early mammals and dinosaurs, members of the reptile family,
appeared on the scene. Dinosaurs, instead of crawling on their
stomachs, stood up and walked on four legs or on two.
A few of the reptiles returned
to a life in the water.

MESOZOIC ERA
[Middle Life]

TRIASSIC
PERIOD

to about 200,000,000 years ago

ACT
II

Scene 1

from about 200,000,000 years ago

ANCIENT
MAMMALS

ANCIENT
BIRD

RHAMPHORYNCHUS
ram·for·ink·us

ORNITHOLESTES
or·nith·o·les·teez

ALLOSAURUS
al·o·sawr·us

APATOSAURUS
a·pat·o·sawr·us

STEGOSAURUS
steg·o·sawr·us

MESOZOIC ERA
[Middle Life]

JURASSIC
PERIOD

Once again the climate was warm and moist.
Some of the plant-eating dinosaurs had grown tremendous.
Some had developed armor for protection from their meat-eating cousins.
Some reptiles had learned how to fly. The first real bird appeared.
Little mammals were present, but they played
a very small part at this time.

to about 145,000,000 years ago

PTERANODON
tear·an·o·don

from about 145,000,000 years ago

PALEOSCINCUS
pale·o·skink·us

Mountains were slowly rising.
Shallow seas flooded the lowlands.
On land, in the sea, and in the air, the reptiles ruled.
Now flowering plants appeared for the first time.

GORGOSAURUS
gor·go·sawr·us

PARASAUROLOPHUS
par·a·sawr·all·of·us

MESOZOIC ERA
[middle life]

LOWER
CRETACEOUS
PERIOD

MOSASAURUS
mo·sa·sawr·us

ELASMOSAURUS
e·laz·mo·sawr·us

PLESIOSAUR
pleez·yo·sawr

to about 100,000,000 years ago

ACT
II
Scene 3

HESPERORNIS
hes·per·orn·is

ARCHELON
ar·kel·on

from about 100,000,000 years ago

STRUTHIOMIMUS
strooth·ee·o·mime·us

Mountains continued to rise.
The climate grew colder and colder. The shallow seas retreated.
On the very last day of this period, a ten-kilometer-wide meteor hit the earth.
This catastrophic event brought about the extinction of species upon species
of dinosaur, never to be seen on Earth again except as fossils
in museums of natural history.

STYRACOSAURUS
sty·rack·o·sawr·us

TRICERATOPS
tri·ser·at·ops

TYRANNOSAURUS
ty·ran·o·sawr·us

CORYTHOSAURUS
kor·ith·o·sawr·us

MESOZOIC ERA
[middle life]

LATE
CRETACEOUS
PERIOD

to about 65,000,000 years

ACT
II
Scene 4

HYRACOTHERIUM
high·ra·co·thee·ree·um
Four-toed dawn horse

from about 65,000,000 years ago

DIATRYMA
dy·artry·ma

PATRIOFELIS
pat·ree·o·feel·is

The scene has changed . . .
The climate had turned hot and humid.
Dense tropical forests covered most of the lowlands.
The few survivors of the reptile family now played a minor role.
The leading roles had been taken over by birds and mammals.
Mammals bear their young alive and take care of them
until they are old enough to take care of themselves.
Both birds and mammals are warm-blooded animals
while all others are cold-blooded.

UINTATHERIUM
yew·in·ta·thee·ree·um

BASILOSAURUS
bass·il·o·sawr·us

Ancient whale

CENOZOIC ER
[Recent Life]

PALEOGENE
PERIOD

PALEOCENE AND
EOCENE EPOCH
[Dawn of Recent]

to about 34,000,000 years a

ACT
III

Scene 1

from about 34,000,000 years ago

MESOHIPPUS
three·toed horse

OREODONTS
o·ree·o·donts

HOPLOPHONEUS
hop·lo·fone·ee·us

Relative of cats, hyenas

TRIGONIAS
try·go·nee·as
Ancient rhinoceros

The climate grew a little cooler and drier.
True grasses increased and spread at this time.
They are members of the great family of flowering plants.
Mammals were developing and experimenting in various forms.
Although they are the ancestors of our present mammals,
it is difficult to recognize some of them.

ARCHAEOTHERIUM
ark·ee·o·thee·ree·um
Ancient pig relative

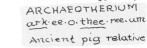

TITANOTHERIUM
ty·tan·o·thee·ree·um

CENOZOIC ERA
[Recent life]

PALEOGENE
PERIOD

OLIGOCENE EPOCH

to about 23,000,000 years ago

ACT
III

Scene 2

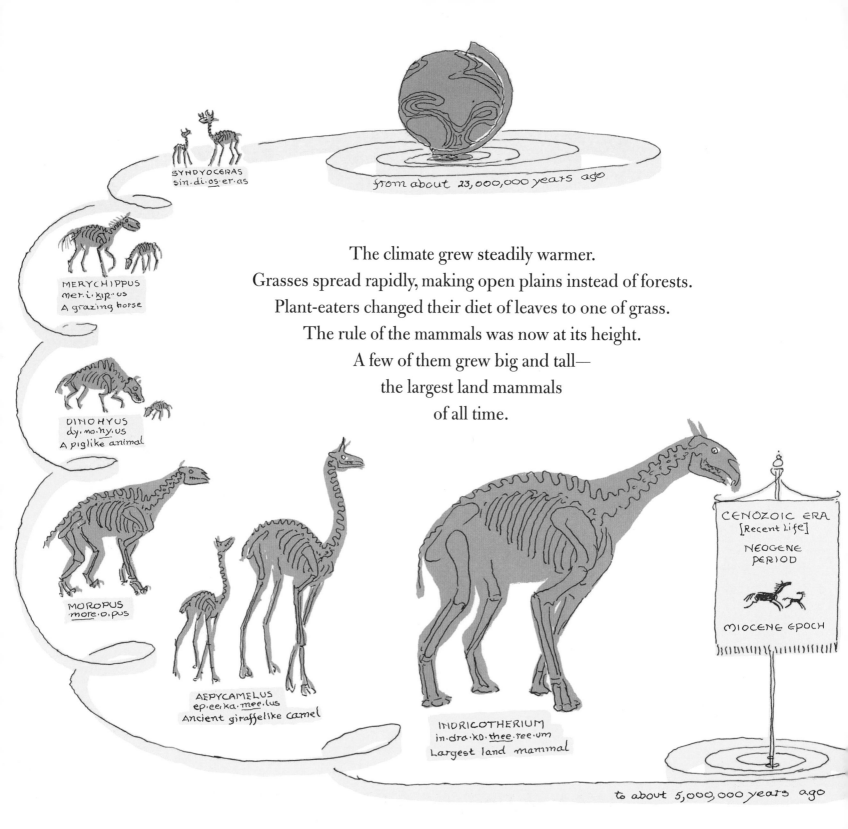

SYNDYOCERAS
sin·di·os·er·as

from about 23,000,000 years ago

MERYCHIPPUS
mer·i·kip·us
A grazing horse

The climate grew steadily warmer.
Grasses spread rapidly, making open plains instead of forests.
Plant-eaters changed their diet of leaves to one of grass.
The rule of the mammals was now at its height.
A few of them grew big and tall—
the largest land mammals
of all time.

DINOHYUS
dy·no·hy·us
A piglike animal

MOROPUS
more·o·pus

AEPYCAMELUS
ep·ee·ka·mee·lus
Ancient giraffelike camel

INDRICOTHERIUM
in·dra·ko·thee·ree·um
Largest land mammal

CENOZOIC ERA
[Recent Life]

NEOGENE
PERIOD

MIOCENE EPOCH

to about 5,000,000 years ago

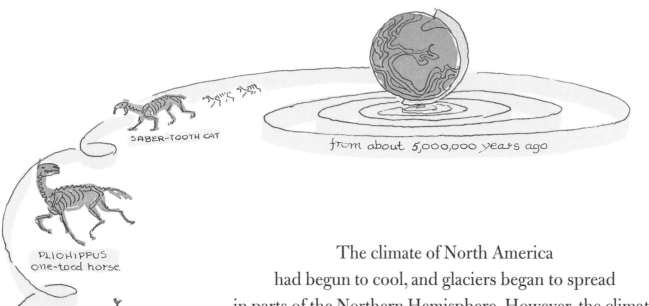

from about 5,000,000 years ago

SABER-TOOTH CAT

PLIOHIPPUS
one-toed horse

SYNTHETOCERAS
sin·the·toe·sair·as

The climate of North America
had begun to cool, and glaciers began to spread
in parts of the Northern Hemisphere. However, the climate
of most of North America and Europe was still fairly warm,
and animal life began to look more like
the mammals we know today.

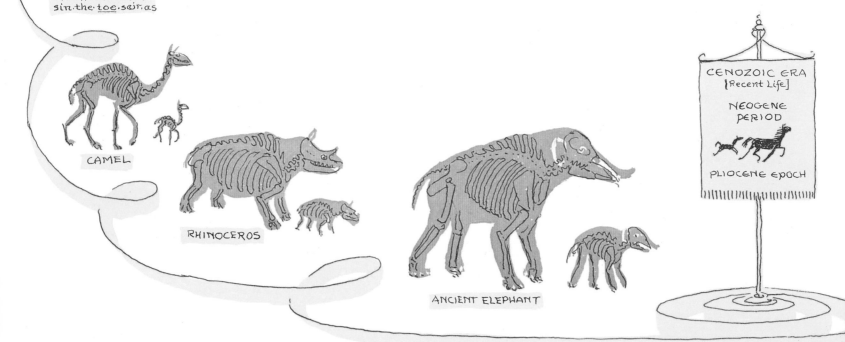

CAMEL

RHINOCEROS

ANCIENT ELEPHANT

CENOZOIC ERA
[Recent Life]

NEOGENE
PERIOD

PLIOCENE EPOCH

To about 1,800,000 years ago

from about 1,800,000 years ago

TERATORNIS
A monstrous bird

ICE AGE HORSE

ICE AGE LION

WOOLLY RHINOCEROS

GIANT CAMEL

WOOLLY MAMMOTH

CENOZOIC ERA
[Recent Life]

QUATERNARY
PERIOD

PLEISTOCENE EPOCH

In the north, great glaciers formed
and slowly moved southward, scraping the land bare.
This time in Life's history on Earth is called the Ice Age.
These great masses of ice advanced and melted and retreated
multiple times. Humans were present at this time
but played a very minor role.

to about 11,000 years ago

ACT
III
Scene 5

from about 11,000 years ago

The appearance of humans on the scene
happened only a short time ago as compared
to the long length of time that all other Life had been present.
Prehistoric humans lived in caves and discovered the use of fire.
They made tools and weapons of stone or pieces of bone.
They hunted the wild animals for food and clothing,
and they painted pictures of these animals
on the walls of caves.

CENOZOIC ERA
QUATERNARY PERIOD

HOLOCENE EPOCH

AGE OF HUMANS

ACT
IV

Scene 1

EGYPT

from about 11,000 years ago

GREECE

ROME

Humans learned how to cultivate
plants and domesticate animals for their own use.
Instead of wandering around and living in caves, they
built houses and lived in villages, towns, and cities. They found
out how to build boats and to sail the high seas. With the
development of languages, recorded history began.
Historians tell the story of the rise and fall of
the great civilizations of the Old World
and the discovery of the New World.

MIDDLE AGES

RENAISSANCE

AGE OF EXPLORATION

NEW ENGLAND

to about 400 years ago

from about 400 years ago

The scene is set in the New World
not long after it was first discovered.
Here the early settlers cleared the land, cutting
down the trees and building log cabins. The many
rocks and boulders left by the glaciers were used to
build stone walls and to divide up the land.
The life of the early settlers
was not an easy one.

to about 200 years ago

from about 200 years ago

When our great-grandparents were young,
our country was mostly a farming country.
The wilderness had been turned into rich farmlands.
The farmer worked hard to make a living from the soil.
He rose early to milk the cows and to feed the livestock.
In the springtime he plowed and planted his crops.
In the summer he cultivated them and made hay,
and in the fall he gathered the harvest
and stored it away for the winter.

To about 100 years ago

ACT
IV

Scene 4

from about a 100 years ago

And now, a few generations later,
the once well-cared-for farms were deserted.
The farmers had either gone west or moved into the cities.
The fields were overgrown with briers, bushes, and trees.
All that remained to show that humans had lived here
were the stone walls dividing the land
and a few old apple trees.

to about 25 years ago

from about 25 years ago

Twenty-five summers have passed quickly
since we bought the old orchard, meadow, and woodland
and moved a little house and my barn studio into the middle of it.
The old apple trees have been trimmed, the woods cleaned up,
and in the meadow we have put sheep to keep the grass down.
Evergreens and flowering plants have been planted.
Ferns and mosses grow by the running brook.
Here is where we raised our children
until they grew old enough to begin
living a life of their own.

to about a year ago

ACT
V

Scene 1

The season has changed from summer to fall.
The days are shorter and the nights are longer.
The air is cooler and the first frost nips the plants,
turning the green leaves to bright red, orange, and yellow
before they are caught by the wind and flutter to the ground.
Only the hardy evergreens are not affected by the cold.
The sap in the trees and shrubs sinks low in the roots—
and the seeds for next year's plants have been shed.
Many birds fly south to escape the winter.

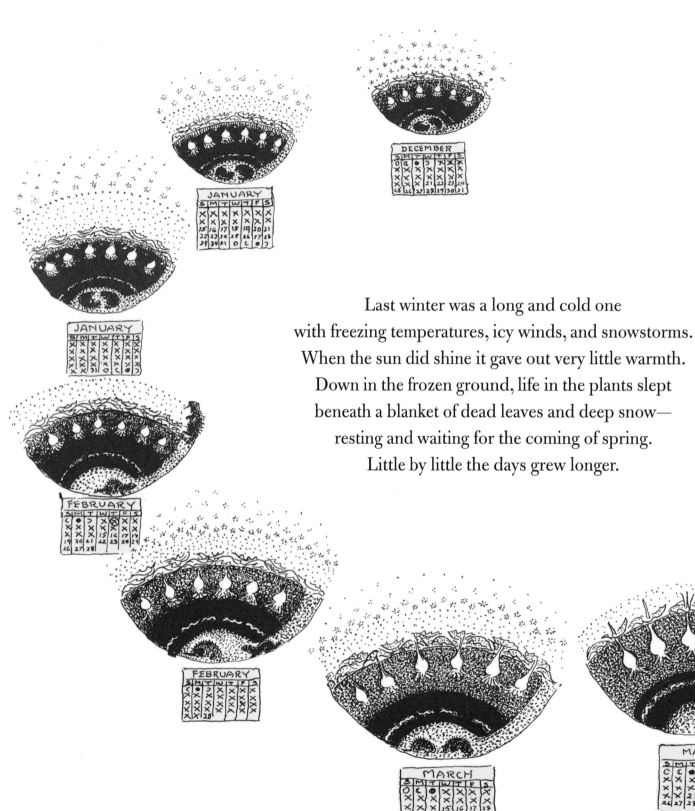

Last winter was a long and cold one
with freezing temperatures, icy winds, and snowstorms.
When the sun did shine it gave out very little warmth.
Down in the frozen ground, life in the plants slept
beneath a blanket of dead leaves and deep snow—
resting and waiting for the coming of spring.
Little by little the days grew longer.

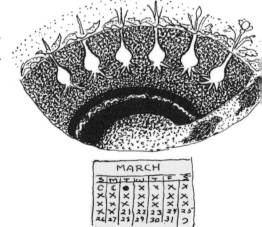

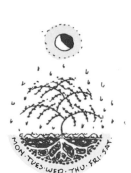

In the first month of spring
the snow melted and the ground thawed.
Day by day, week by week, the grass grew greener.
Gentle showers encouraged the early spring flowers.
In the trees the sap was rising, swelling the new buds.
Under the ground last year's seeds began to stir and awaken,
pushing tender shoots up through the earth and dead leaves,
reaching up for the light and warmth of the sun.
The birds returned from the south.

Yesterday was a day to remember—
one of those beautiful warm spring days
when one could almost see the plants growing.
Lowly little lichens clinging to the rocks brightened,
liverworts and velvety mosses carpeted the damp ground,
ferns pushed up and unfurled their delicate fronds,
new bright green needles tipped the evergreens,
buds opened and tiny little leaves unfolded,
and the apple trees burst into blossom.
In the meadow the sheep grazed happily
on the tender new shoots of grass.
The miracle of spring was here.

VI

VII

VIII

IX

X

XI

XII

ACT
V

Scene 5

As the afternoon hours slipped by
and the sun began to sink in the west,
the shadows on the ground gradually lengthened.
Just before the sun set it turned fiery red,
tinting the sky and the earth bright pink.
High overhead a pale new moon appeared.
By the brook the frogs were singing
their song of spring.

ACT
V

Scene 6

The new moon had set
and darkness had fallen.
One by one the stars had come out—
millions and billions of stars, trillions of miles away.
The Big Dipper hung high in the bright spring sky,
pointing out the steady-standing North Star.
Low on the horizon gleamed the Milky Way.
Inside the house, the hands of the clock
showed that another day had passed
and a new day had begun.

ACT
V

Scene 7

And now it is dawn—
dawn of a new day, a day in the spring.
Minute by minute the light brightens in the east,
turning from cold gray to deep blue to delicate pink.
The birds are singing gaily as they await the return of the sun.
Down in the green meadow there is a new baby lamb.
Now I leave you and turn the story over to you.
Look out your window and in a few seconds
you will see the sun rise.

ACT
V

Scene 8

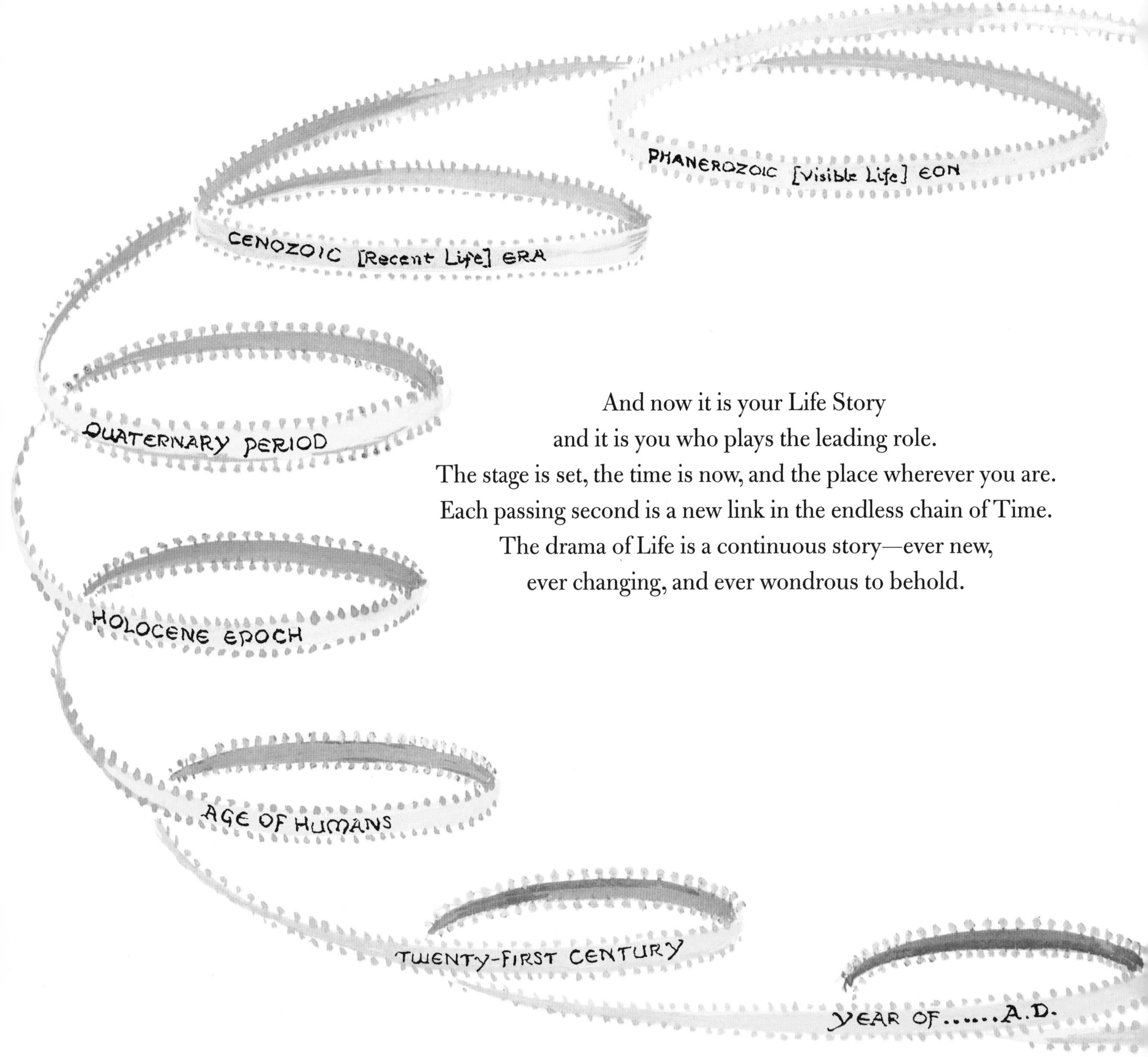

PHANEROZOIC [Visible Life] EON

CENOZOIC [Recent Life] ERA

QUATERNARY PERIOD

HOLOCENE EPOCH

AGE OF HUMANS

TWENTY-FIRST CENTURY

YEAR OF......A.D.

And now it is your Life Story
and it is you who plays the leading role.
The stage is set, the time is now, and the place wherever you are.
Each passing second is a new link in the endless chain of Time.
The drama of Life is a continuous story—ever new,
ever changing, and ever wondrous to behold.

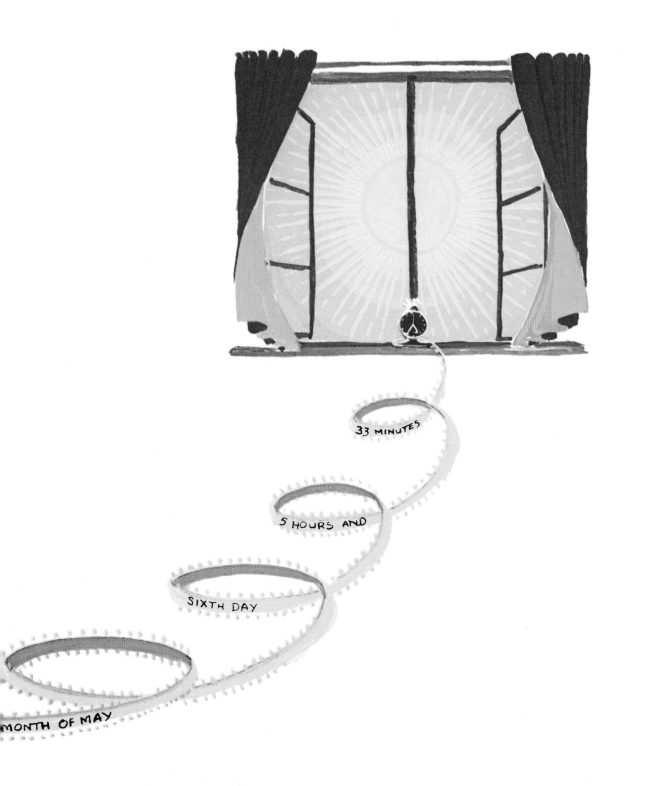

33 MINUTES

5 HOURS AND

SIXTH DAY

MONTH OF MAY